THE WING ON A FLEA

a book about shapes

by Ed Emberley

 LITTLE, BROWN AND COMPANY

New York ~ Boston

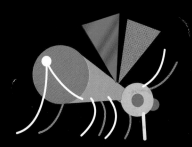

A triangle could be the wing on a flea

or the beak on a bird, if you'll just look and see.

A bandit's bandana,   an admiral's hat,

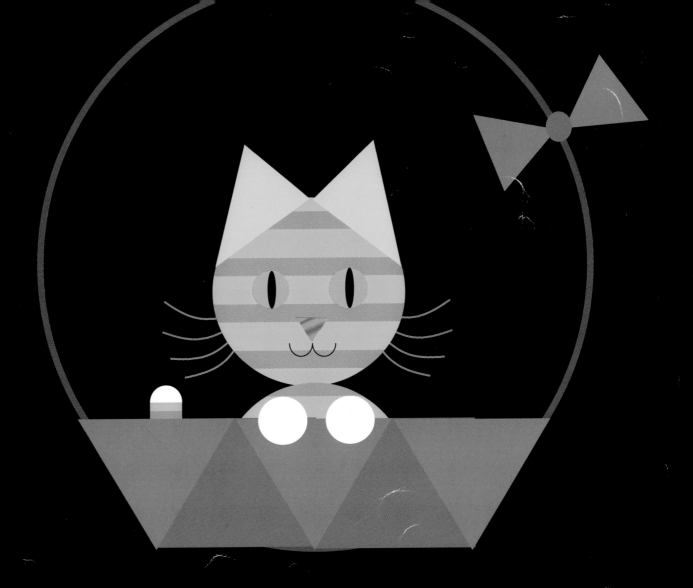

and, in case you don't know it, the nose on a cat.

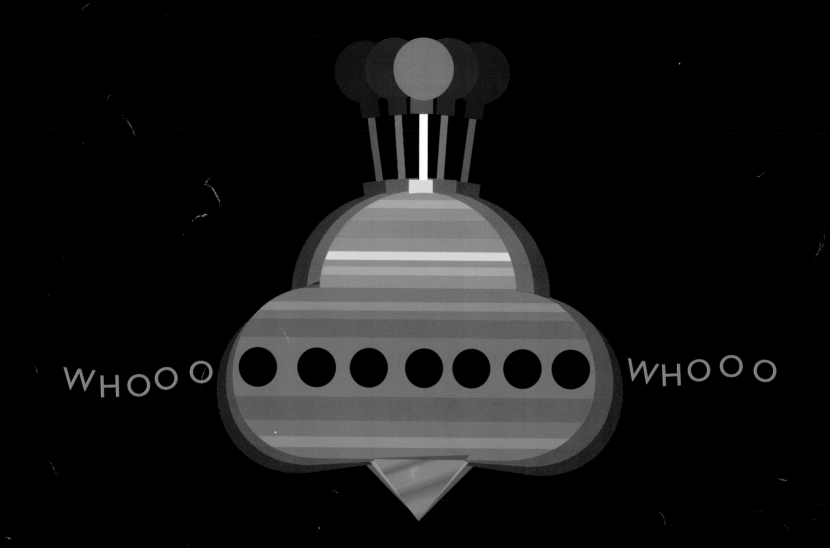

WHOOO   WHOOO

The tip of a top,

a tepee or tree.

You'll find lots around, if you'll just look and see.

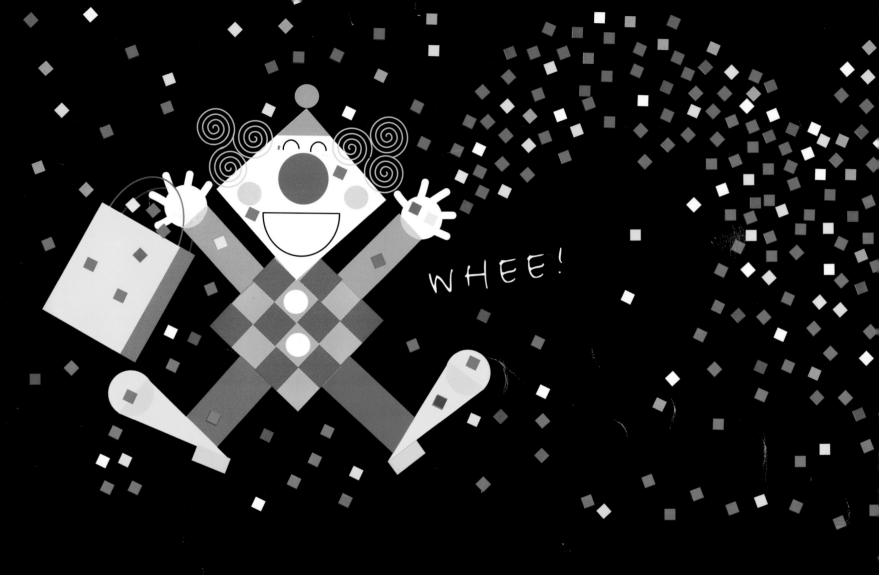

WHEE!

A rectangle could be, if you'll just look and see,

a piece of confetti to throw and say, "Whee!"

A bandage for boo-boos, a ruler to measure,

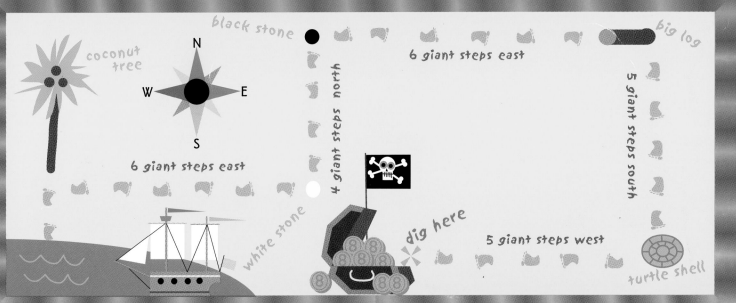

coconut tree

black stone

big log

N

W   E

S

6 giant steps east

5 giant steps south

6 giant steps east

4 giant steps north

white stone

dig here

5 giant steps west

turtle shell

the map pirates use to find buried treasure

BLIX
BLOX

Joseph Blix and Son
By appointment,
makers of fine wooden blocks
for H.R.H. King Cole.

a bag full of tea.

WELCOME

You'll find lots around, if you'll just look and see.

A circle could be a little green pea,

or eyes in the dark, if you'll just look and see.

A marble, a bubble,

a ball, a balloon.

The earth and the sun,

and sometimes the moon.

The wheels on a train, the hole in a key.

You'll find lots around, if you'll just look and see.

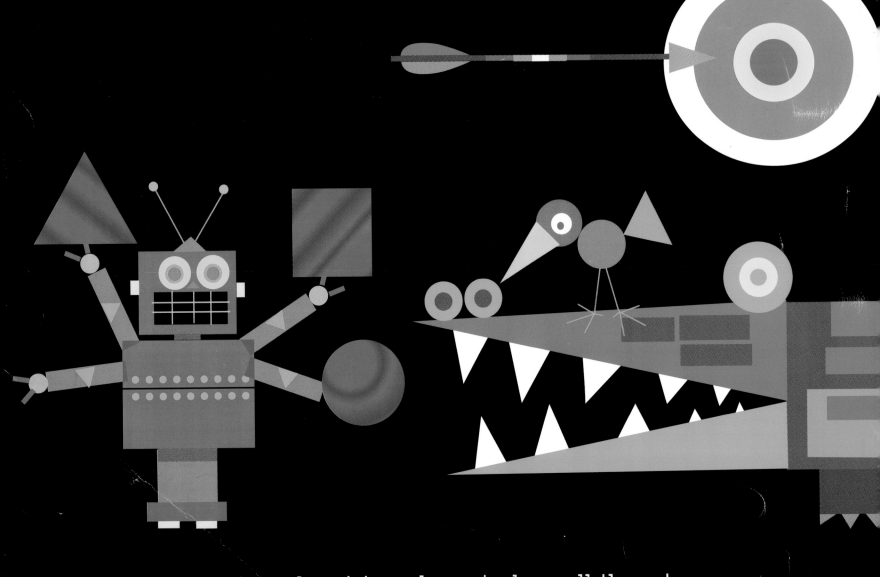

Rectangles, triangles, circles, all three!

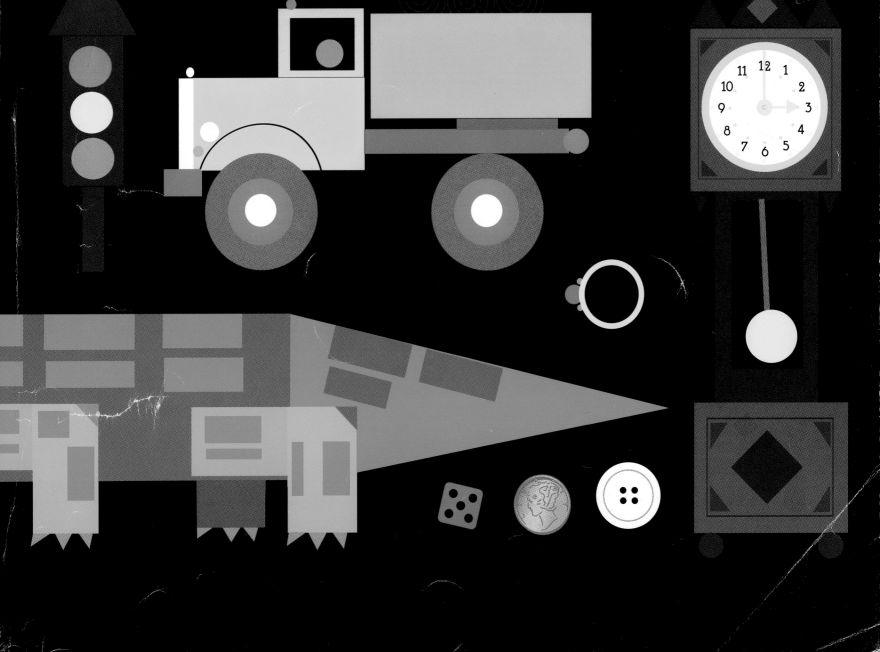

On the envelope:

Thomas Thumb
Over the Hills
and Far Away

Princess Thumbelina
Copenhagen
Denmark

On the gum wrapper: YUMMY GUM

You'll find lots around, if ---'-- ---- ---- --- ---.

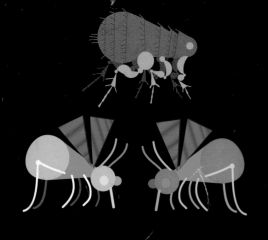

Real fleas have no wings and come in various shades of gray.

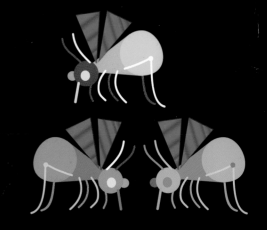

My make-believe fleas have wings and come in many colors.

Can you find the real flea?

Circles, rectangles, triangles, and a few lines and scribbles were used to make the pictures in this book.

Can you see how these parts were used to make this clown?

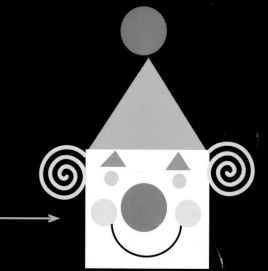

While this book is meant to stand on its own, it also serves as an introduction to a series of drawing books that show how to make your own pictures using simple shapes and a few scribbles, dots, and lines.

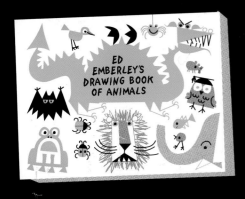

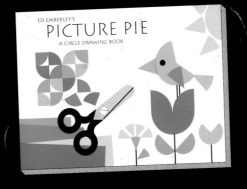

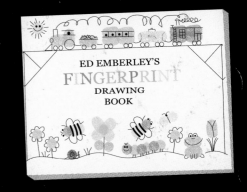

The Drawing Book series shows how to make pictures using these shapes.

The Picture Pie series shows how to make pictures using cut-and-paste circles.

The Fingerprint series shows how to make pictures from finger- and thumbprints.

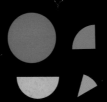

Little, Brown and Company

Hachette Book Group USA
1271 Avenue of the Americas, New York, NY 10020
Visit our Web site at www.lb-kids.com

First Edition

ISBN 0-316-23487-7
LCCN 00-049725

10   9   8   7   6   5   4   3

TWP

Printed in Singapore

Dedications

Sixty-four years ago, in 1937, my first-grade teacher, Miss Dance, came up behind me, looked at the picture I was drawing and said, "Humm, nice boat." That was it, I have loved boats and drawing ever since. Thanks you, Miss Dance.

Forty years ago, in 1961, the first version of *The Wing on a Flea* was published. It was my first picture book, just one of many different jobs that came across my desk that year, but it was the job I loved the most. Forty years and more than one hundred books later, it is still the job I love the most.

Thank you, everybody